The Sleeping Beauty
in the Wood

Retold and Illustrated by
Carol Heyer

Ideals Children's Books • Nashville, Tennessee
an imprint of Hambleton-Hill Publishing, Inc.

Once upon a time, in a land still touched by magic, there lived a king and a queen whose fondest wish was to have a child of their own. They sought out every wise man in the kingdom and tried every potion, but still there was no child.

One day, as the queen was out walking, she paused by the edge of a wishing pool. Closing her eyes, she wished once again her fondest wish. She then slipped off her golden ring and tossed it into the deep, still waters. The instant the ring touched the surface, the water began to churn and an enormous frog sprang out before her.

The creature bowed deeply and said in a rumbling, watery voice, "Good Queen, because your wish is heartfelt, it shall be granted. With the coming of the spring, you shall have a daughter." This said, the great frog bowed again, turned, and jumped back into the wishing pool, vanishing as suddenly as he had appeared.

The frog's prediction came true, and that very spring the queen gave birth to a beautiful baby girl. The king and queen were overjoyed, and indeed every person in every corner of the kingdom rejoiced with them. At once, the king began making plans for a grand christening feast, inviting everyone from near and far to attend.

At the request of the king, the princess had for her godmothers all the fairies that could be found in the kingdom. Seven were found in all, and each fairy was personally invited to the christening so that she might bestow a magical gift upon the child.

The day of the christening arrived, and after the ceremonies the guests returned to the castle for a feast. The great hall was filled with people and at the royal table sat the seven fairy godmothers. The banquet was as splendid as any that had ever been seen. In honor of the special day, the king gave each fairy godmother a place setting made of the purest gold.

After the feast, the fairies gathered around the princess. The first one touched her cheek and wished her great beauty; the second touched her forehead and wished for her the wit of an angel; the third touched the crown of her head and wished that she should have grace in everything she did; the fourth touched her feet and wished that she should dance perfectly well; the fifth brushed her throat and wished that she should sing like a nightingale; and the sixth fairy held her hand and wished that she should play all kinds of musical instruments to the utmost perfection.

But before the seventh fairy could bestow her gift, there was a rumbling from deep within the earth and the very foundations of the castle began to shake. Suddenly the doors to the great hall burst open. A cloud of sulfureous smoke exploded into the hall and from the darkness hobbled an ancient crone.

The guests gasped to see her, for the old fairy had not been seen for more than fifty years, and she was believed by all to be either dead or enchanted. Yet here she was, feeling very slighted indeed that she had not been invited to the feast nor been given a golden plate like her fairy sisters.

The old fairy hobbled past the king and queen, past all the guests, past the castle guard, past the terrified servants, and past her fairy sisters to the princess in her crib. The evil fairy placed her twisted fingers over the baby's heart and said in a horrible, cackling voice, "When the child reaches her sixteenth year, she shall prick her finger on the spindle of a spinning wheel and die!" With her curse echoing through the hall, the old crone disappeared in a burst of smoke and flame.

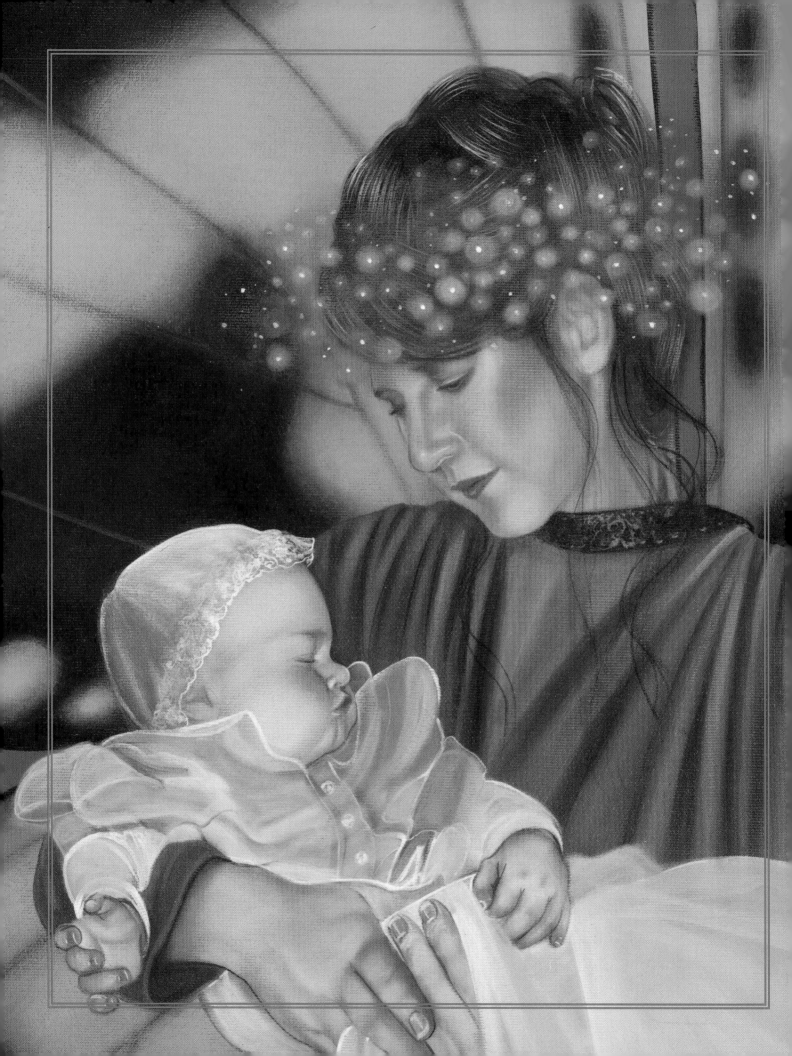

The king was horrified, the entire company despaired, and as the queen began to cry, the seventh fairy stepped forward, cradling the tiny princess in her arms. "It is true, I cannot undo all of the evil spell. The princess shall indeed pierce her hand with a spindle, but she shall not die. Instead, she shall fall into a deep sleep that shall last one hundred years. At the end of that time, the touch of a royal prince shall awaken her."

The king and queen took some comfort from the fairy's words, but still they worried for their child. A proclamation was sent throughout the kingdom, ordering that all spinning wheels and spindles be destroyed. And so, on that very day, in the village square, every spinning wheel and every spindle in the entire kingdom was burned. The king and queen watched until the fire burned down to embers and then to ashes that were carried away by the winds. Only then did they return to the castle.

The years passed and, as the princess grew, all the gifts of her fairy godmothers were fulfilled. The princess was more beautiful, more polite, more sensible and kind, than anyone could have wished, and all who chanced to meet her could not help but adore her.

As her sixteenth birthday drew near, the entire castle was in a state of excited confusion as they prepared for the celebration. Wherever the princess went, she was shooed away for fear she might see their surprises.

At a loss for something to do, she began to wander into the little used corners of the castle, visiting rooms she had never before seen. Her wanderings eventually led her to an ancient, marbled tower. She climbed the winding staircase to the top and found a wooden door. It creaked softly as she pushed it open. Inside there sat an old woman at her spinning wheel, busily spinning flax.

Having never seen a spinning wheel, the princess stared in wonder and asked, "What are you doing there, dear lady?"

"I'm spinning flax into thread, child, so that I may weave a cloth for your birthday gown," replied the old woman. "Would you like to come closer and try for yourself?"

The princess smiled and stretched her hand toward the wheel, but the spindle seemed to come alive, jumping from its place to prick her finger. The princess snatched back her hand, but it was too late. The evil spell had already begun. She sank back upon a bed that was standing nearby and slipped into a deep, enchanted sleep.

The old woman sprang to her feet and threw off her disguise, revealing herself to be the evil fairy. To her, it was as if her curse had been fulfilled and death, not sleep, had overtaken the girl. With a wicked laugh, the old fairy disappeared.

The sleep that claimed the princess quickly spread throughout the entire castle. It touched the king and queen on their thrones, the servants at their tasks, the guards at the gate, and the cooks in the kitchen. It blanketed the horses in the stable, the dogs in the courtyard, and the birds on the roof. Even the fire flickering in the hearth became quiet. Everyone and everything fell into a deep sleep.

When all was still, briars began to grow all around the castle. They grew and grew and tangled themselves into an ever-thickening wood until only the tallest towers of the castle could be seen, and those only from a great distance.

The princess came to be known as the Sleeping Beauty, and tales of her enchanted castle were told throughout the land. As her legend grew, so grew the thorns in the briar wood, until they were as large and as sharp as daggers. Over the years, many princes tried to reach the castle, but all failed and few returned. So the barrier remained and the princess slept undisturbed.

At long last a wandering prince from a distant
kingdom rode by the briar wood. He wondered about
the castle towers that rose up behind the thick forest,
and he stopped often to question the villagers he
passed. But the princess had been sleeping for so long
that the townspeople had forgotten the true story, and
most now believed that the castle belonged to an ogre.

The prince then happened upon the oldest man in
the village. He told the prince a story that his father's
father had once told him of a beautiful princess who
lay sleeping in the tallest tower of the castle. An evil
spell had been cast upon this princess, causing her to
sleep for one hundred years. Only after the hundred
years had passed could the spell be broken, and then
only by the touch of a royal prince.

Then and there, the prince decided that he would be the one to rescue the princess. The old man warned him of the danger, telling him of all the others who had tried to reach the princess and were lost. But the prince was not afraid, and the old man could say nothing to change his mind.

Though no one knew it, that very day marked the end of the hundred years of the fairy's evil spell. So as the prince approached the briar wood, it opened before him and allowed him to pass through unharmed. Instead of ripping thorns, the softest of flower petals brushed his face. The wood then closed behind him, again forming a thorny wall so that no others could follow.

Inside the castle courtyard, the prince stared at the horses and dogs that lay scattered about in their sleep. He looked up to see the birds in the trees still frozen in their song. When he entered the castle, he found the entire court just as they had been on that day one hundred years ago. The servants stood sleeping at their tasks, the guards snored at their posts, and the king and queen dozed in splendor upon their throne. The prince shivered at the strange sights but continued his search for the sleeping princess.

At last, he found the winding staircase that led to the top of the tallest tower. His steps quickened as he climbed higher and higher until finally he reached the tower chamber.

The door was still open and, when the prince looked inside, he saw the Sleeping Beauty. He marveled that the years of sleep had not dulled her beauty. Her cheeks were still a rosy pink, her skin a glowing cream, and her hair was a glorious, shimmering black. He walked over to the bed, leaned over, and kissed her gently. As his lips touched her cheek, the Sleeping Beauty awoke at last.

She knew the prince in an instant, for though the princess had been sleeping for a hundred years, the good fairy had filled her sleep with dreams of her handsome rescuer. She took his face between her hands and looked at him fondly.

Hand in hand, the prince and princess left the tower chamber. The spell of sleep continued to drift away, and gradually the entire castle began to rouse from its slumber—first the king and queen, then one by one their court and the servants below. The guards snapped to attention, the animals in the courtyard scurried about, and the birds resumed their songs. The forest of briars and thorns disappeared, and everything was as it had been.

As the company gathered in the great hall, the enchanted frog appeared before them. He carried with him a golden ring—the same ring that the queen had tossed into the wishing pool so long ago. And on that day, it became a wedding ring as the Sleeping Beauty and her prince were married in the castle's chapel.

Once again the kingdom rejoiced, and they all lived happily ever after in this land of enchantment and grace.

History of the Story

Variations of the story of Sleeping Beauty have been traced back to fourteenth-century Scandinavia and France. The first published versions appeared in Italy in the sixteenth and seventeenth centuries, but they were intended for a more adult audience. The most widely known versions of the story are those written by Charles Perrault and the Brothers Grimm. Perrault's work, based on popular folklore, was first published in France in 1697 in a collection of fairy tales entitled *Contes de ma mere l'oye* or *Tales of Mother Goose*. The Brothers Grimm published their version in Germany in 1812. The primary difference between the two works lies in the ending. In Perrault's tale, the prince's mother is an ogress who tries to have Sleeping Beauty and her children killed so she can eat them for dinner! The Brothers Grimm chose to end the story on a happier note—with the marriage of Sleeping Beauty to her handsome rescuer.

In creating her own adaptation of the tale, Carol Heyer drew upon its rich history, interweaving elements of the original Perrault and Brothers Grimm works with her own imaginative additions, making *The Sleeping Beauty in the Wood* a captivating new classic.

Published by Ideals Children's Books
An imprint of Hambleton-Hill Publishing, Inc.
Nashville, Tennessee 37218

Printed and bound in Mexico

Library of Congress Cataloging-in-Publication Data
Heyer, Carol, 1950–
    The sleeping beauty in the wood / retold and illustrated by Carol Heyer.
        p.   cm.
    Summary: Enraged at not being invited to the princess' christening, the wicked fairy casts a spell that dooms the princess to sleep for one hundred years.
    ISBN 1-57102-094-2
    [1. Fairy Tales. 2. Folklore—Germany.] 1. Sleeping Beauty. English. II. Title.
PZ8.H48SI   1996
398.2'0943'02–dc20   96-16133
[E]   CIP
                                                    AC

First Edition

10 9 8 7 6 5 4 3 2 1

For my Aunt Ailsa Hutson.
For my parents, William J. Heyer and Merlyn Heyer,
now and always.
                                                    —C. H.

Special thanks to models:
Claire Benham . . . . .Sleeping Beauty
Jeff Hoover . . . . .Prince
Suzan Davis Atkinson .Pink Fairy
Andrea Rosenstein . . . . .Blue Fairy
Mary Jean Sumell . . . . .Purple Fairy
Oceana Marr . . . . .Housekeeper
Barbara Cogswell . . . . .Queen
David Atkinson . . . . .King
Baby Atkinson . . . . .Sleeping Beauty Infant
Blake Beckman . . . . .Trumpeter
Logan Rosenstein . . . . .Page
J. J., T. C., & Tinker Bell . . . . .Members of the Court

The illustrations in this book were rendered in acrylic on canvas using live models.
The text type was set in Bandicoot.
The display type was set in Ermine.
Color separations were made by Color 4, Inc.
Printed and bound by R.R. Donnelley & Sons Company.